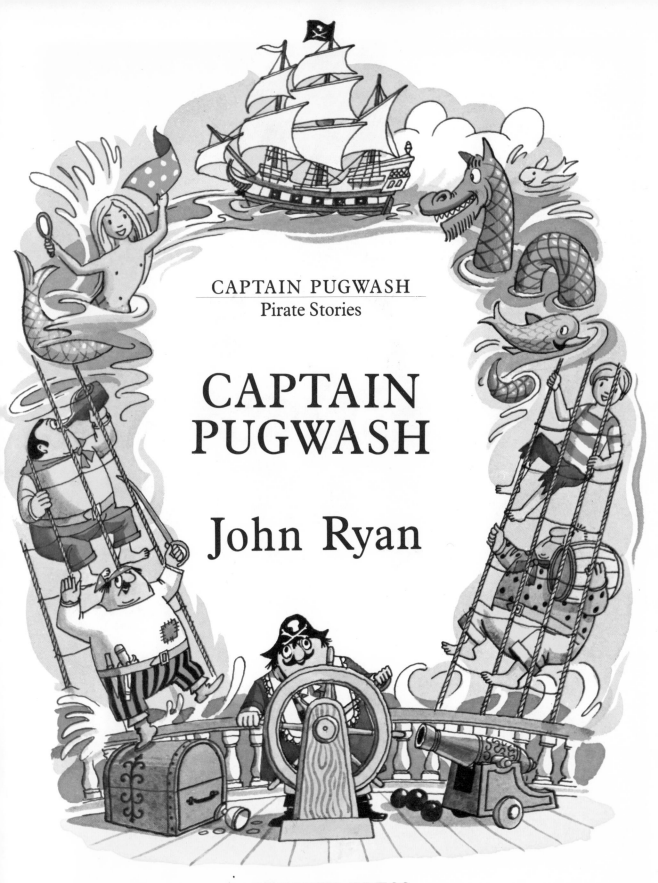

CAPTAIN PUGWASH
Pirate Stories

CAPTAIN
PUGWASH

John Ryan

CRESSET PRESS
London Sydney Auckland Johannesburg

Captain Pugwash was a pirate. He thought himself the bravest, most handsome pirate on the seven seas. Here is a portrait of him.

He had a ship called *The Black Pig*, with
a crew that was the laziest afloat, and a
Mate who was always fast asleep.

He had, too, a cabin boy called Tom, and this was lucky, because Tom was really the only person aboard who knew how to work the compass, sail the ship, and make the tea.

One sunny morning, Captain Pugwash was happily steering his ship through the blue Caribbean Sea, looking, as usual, for treasure. The mate was asleep, of course, and the crew were all busy . . .

lying about the deck,
playing games,
and watching the clouds
and the waves
and the
fishes.

The Captain had a map

to show him where the treasure was
and to help him to steer clear of sea monsters and storms.

The only thing that really worried Captain Pugwash was the danger of meeting other pirates. One of these, whose name was Cut-throat Jake, was so fierce that the very thought of him was enough to make Captain Pugwash want to give up sailing and take to market gardening instead.

Cut-throat Jake was a very bad man indeed. Everyone said that his heart was blacker than his beard. He had an enormous ship, bristling with guns, and worst of all, he simply hated Captain Pugwash.

The Captain was just thinking about this when there was a loud cry from the crow's nest, where Tom, who was keeping a look-out with his telescope, had just spotted a ship.

'SHIP AHOY!' shouted Tom—so loudly that it made the Captain jump, and almost woke up the mate.

'What sort of ship?' cried Captain Pugwash, rushing anxiously to the side. 'Does it look like a treasure ship?'

'It looks a funny sort of ship to me,' said Tom as he climbed down the rigging.

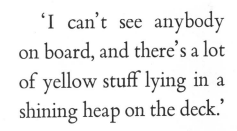

'I can't see anybody on board, and there's a lot of yellow stuff lying in a shining heap on the deck.'

'What!' shouted the Captain, seizing the telescope. 'Good gracious me—it's TREASURE—and no one to guard it! Lower the dinghy—I'm going aboard!'

'All by yourself, Cap'n?' said Tom. 'And why not, boy?' said Pugwash. 'There's nobody to fight, and besides, if I go alone, all the treasure will belong to me.'

'Please, Cap'n,' said Tom, 'Wouldn't it be safer if I went too? I shan't want any of the treasure, and—well you know *you* aren't very good at rowing . . .'

'Oh, very well,' grunted the Captain.

It was never easy getting him out of a big boat into a small one, but in the end they managed it, and away they went.

Over on the other ship, Cut-throat Jake
laughed softly into his enormous beard, and
waited . . .

For years he had been trying to catch Pugwash. He had never succeeded because the Captain was so frightened of him that he always ran away long before Jake could get anywhere near him. Then Jake had suddenly thought of a wonderful plan. He had disguised his ship and waited for *The Black Pig* to come near. Then he had scattered gold and precious stones all over the deck, and hidden himself and his crew.

✳   ✳   ✳   ✳

'Faster, boy! Faster!' cried the Captain as Tom rowed closer and closer to the strange ship.

At last they reached it. A rope ladder was hanging conveniently over the side, and Pugwash heaved himself on to the deck. And when he got there, he could hardly believe his eyes.

There was gold and silver and precious
stones galore and, waiting down below,
Tom could hear the Captain's exclamations
of delight as he gazed at the sparkling
treasure.

Then, suddenly, Tom heard a different
sort of noise . . .

'Yo ho, ho ho!' shouted Cut-throat Jake
as he rushed out from behind a huge coil of rope.

'Ya ha, ha ha!' yelled Jake's pirates,
leaping out of all the hatchways in sight.

And—'HELP!' cried Pugwash in a very
weak voice, as they grabbed him.

'Got you at last!' said Jake. 'Even if it has taken me twenty years. Now, men— what shall we do with him?'

'The plank! The plank! Make him walk the plank!' shouted all the pirates together.

'And a very good idea too,' said Jake. 'And since you're so fond of treasure, Cap'n, we'll fill your pockets with the stuff. It will make you sink more quickly.'

So they stuffed poor Pugwash's pockets
with gold and silver and precious stones,
and filled his boots too, to make him heavier
still. Then they pushed him on to the
plank, and the Captain wished very much
that he had never gone to sea.

But there was one thing
he and Jake and all the
pirates on Jake's ship had
forgotten—and that was
Tom, waiting down below
in the little rowing boat.

'Off you go, Cap'n,'
aid Jake, 'It was so nice
of you to drop in.' And
Pugwash started to totter
very unsteadily along the
plank. If there was one
thing he hated it was cold
water.

'Go on,' shouted Jake,
'Hurry up! We can't wait
all day, you know.'

Pugwash hesitated,
held his nose,
lost his balance,
and toppled off the end
of the plank . . .

'That's the last time you'll drop in anywhere!' shouted Cut-throat Jake—and all the pirates thought this such a good joke that they sat down and roared with laughter for about five minutes. In fact, they were all so busy laughing that none of them saw what really happened. When Pugwash landed in the water, Tom was ready for him, and he pulled the Captain head-first into the dinghy and rowed away as fast as he could.

So when Jake went to the side of the
ship to have another look, this is what he saw.

And when he saw it, he was so angry that he almost burst with rage, and used such terribly bad language that even the wickedest of his crew blushed. 'Get out the cannon!' roared Jake; but as all the cannon and cannon-balls and gunpowder had been hidden, it was a long time before the pirates were ready to fire.

The first shot missed and the second and third shots missed, and then Cut-throat Jake got so angry that he chose an extra large cannon-ball, to make quite sure of hitting the little boat this time.

But . . .

it was too big.

It stuck in the cannon, and when they let it off, the whole thing exploded with a fearful bang which knocked Cut-throat Jake and all his crew senseless.

Meanwhile, aboard *The Black Pig*, Captain Pugwash's pirates were roused by the sudden noise, and rushed to see what was happening.

'It's the Cap'n!' shouted the Mate, rubbing the sleep from his eyes. 'Stand by with the boat-hook!'

So Captain Pugwash came back to his ship again
and stood in triumph on his own quarter-
deck, and *The Black Pig* sailed away as fast
as possible from Cut-throat Jake's ship.

'Smart work, eh,' said the Captain to
his admiring crew, as they watched him
emptying all the treasure which Jake had
given him.

'That old ruffian thought he'd caught
me, but I was too clever for him! Ha!
It takes more than a silly scallywag like
Cut-throat Jake to catch me.'

'Oh well,' thought Tom to himself, as he curled up to sleep in his hammock that night—'It's lucky there was *somebody* there to catch him!'

The End

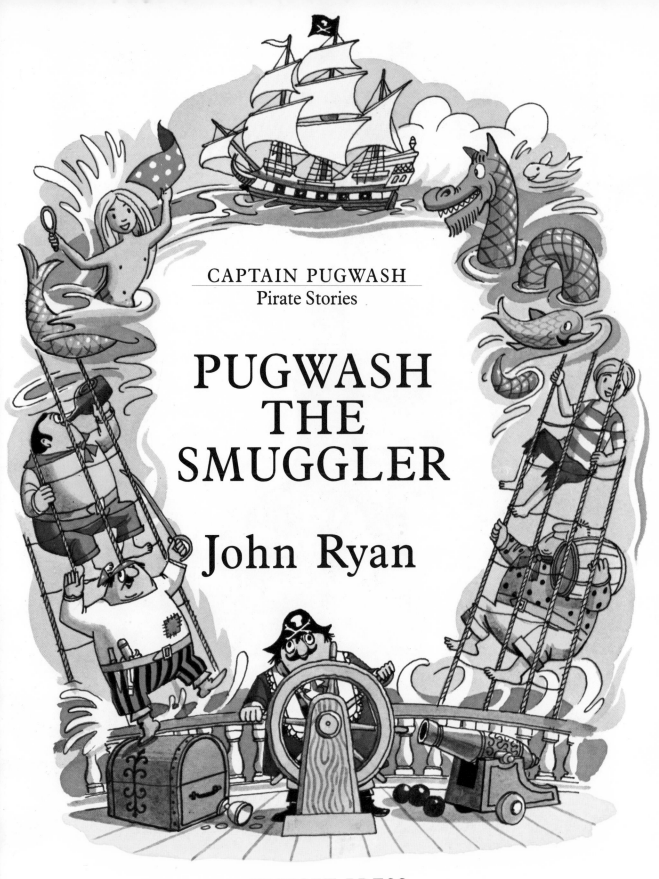

CAPTAIN PUGWASH
Pirate Stories

PUGWASH THE SMUGGLER

John Ryan

CRESSET PRESS

London Sydney Auckland Johannesburg

"Best French brandy, eh?" said Captain Pugwash. "Those four barrels are full of the stuff and you want *me* to load 'em aboard my ship in one hour's time and sail 'em to England?" "*Exactement*, Monsieur," replied his companion. "Deliver them safely, and you will receive five hundred golden crowns!"

The light was fading as the two men stood together on the quayside of a small French sea-port. The second man was an inn-keeper, and above them the sign of the "Golden Fish" creaked and swung in the wind which that night would carry the *Black Pig* across the English Channel.

"Excellent!" said the Captain. "I had no idea smuggling was so well paid. I'll be off to fetch the rest of my crew and we'll be home and dry by morning!" And the two men shook hands.

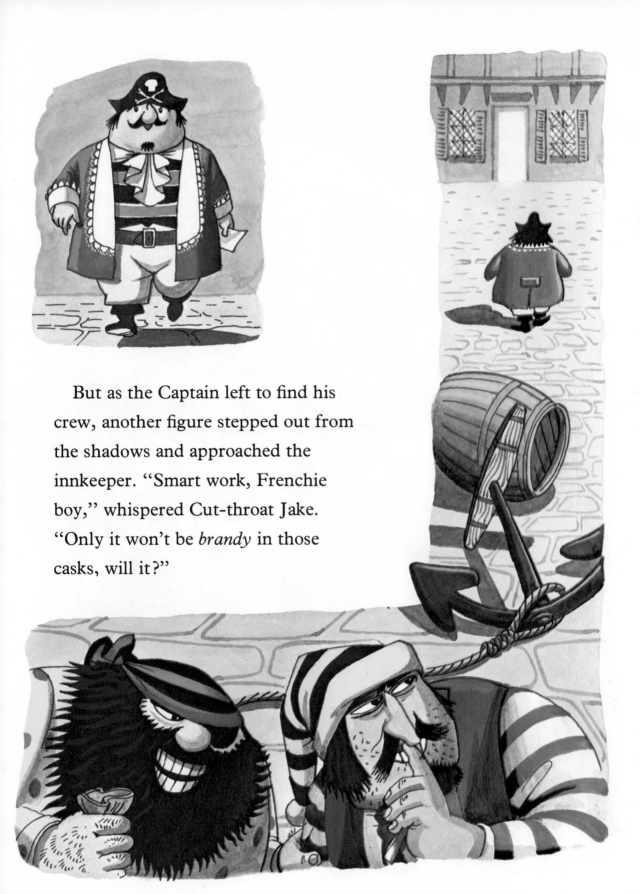

But as the Captain left to find his crew, another figure stepped out from the shadows and approached the innkeeper. "Smart work, Frenchie boy," whispered Cut-throat Jake. "Only it won't be *brandy* in those casks, will it?"

"*Non, non!*" answered the Frenchman, greedily catching the bag of gold which Jake tossed over to him. "You are too kind, Captain Cut-throat!"

"Ho-ho-ho-ho! Kindness is my second name." Jake beckoned to the rest of his ugly crew to join him. "Right, me handsomes. We all know what comes next, don't we?"

An hour or so later,
the *Black Pig* slipped out
of the port and began
the Channel crossing.
The barrels were stowed
safely in the hold . . .

. . . the mate
was at the
wheel . . .

Willie and Barnabas snored in their hammocks below . . .

. . . and Tom the Cabin-boy settled the Captain for the night with a candle, a hot water bottle, a good book and a steaming cup of cocoa.

PIRATE STORIES

PIRATE STORIES by John Ryan

"Ha-ha! this is money for old rope—or should I say old brandy?" chuckled Pugwash. "But you'd better nip down to the hold and make sure everything's ship-shape, Tom."

Meanwhile, in the hold, things were *far* from
ship-shape!

"Open up, all of 'ee," whispered Cut-throat
Jake, and one by one the lid of each brandy barrel
opened to reveal a member of Jake's gang inside.

Tom had arrived in time to hear Jake outlining his plan to seize the ship . . .

but he kept well out of sight so that none of the ruffians realised that they had been overheard.

Then he strolled into the hold as though nothing
was amiss, and picking up a hammer and some nails,

he went over to the
barrels. Just
then the
Captain
called down to ask
if all was well.

"Aye aye,
Cap'n," shouted
Tom, "but some
of the deck planks
are loose. I'm just
going to nail them
down."

EVERYTHING
ALL RIGHT
DOWN THERE,
TOM ?

Of course it wasn't the planks that Tom was nailing down! It was the barrels!

But the pirates inside each barrel thought it *was* the planks . . .

until it came to their turn to be trapped . . .

and by then it was too late.

It was still dark when the *Black Pig* nosed her way into the remote English cove where Pugwash had been instructed to deliver his cargo. He looked at the paper the Frenchman had given him.

"There's a light up there. That must be the place," he said. "Row the barrels ashore, me hearties."

Very soon the pirates had unloaded the four great casks onto the beach.

"Now, up the cliff path," said Pugwash.

"Two to a barrel and we'll have to make two trips. And be as quiet as the grave! We must *not* disturb the Excise Men!"

But the journey up the cliff was not at all quiet. All sorts of strange, angry noises were coming from the barrels.

The crew were blaming each other for the noise, and they were getting very cross and then making more noise than ever. They really didn't know *what* was happening.

Nor did they know that at the top of the cliff, a party of dragoons, specially trained to catch smugglers, was waiting for them.

"Hah! They're walking straight into our trap," whispered the Lieutenant in charge. "Wait for my command, lads." And a moment later . . .

. . . the soldiers rushed out from their hiding place.
Poor Captain Pugwash and his crew were surrounded.

There was no escape as the officer in charge
stepped forward in triumph.

"Caught red-handed! Rascally brandy smugglers, every one of you! Put your barrels down and your hands up! And *you*," he added, pointing to the Captain, "you're the ringleader by the look of it. You're under arrest!"

 Then Tom spoke up. "Please, sir," he said, "we're not smugglers. We've got two notorious pirates in those casks and there are two more down on the beach."

"Pirates, fiddlesticks!" shouted the officer. "Never heard such a tale in me . . ." But at that moment a furious shout came from one of the barrels.

LEMME OUT!!

"By thunder! Maybe the boy's right," cried the
Lieutenant. "Open 'em up!"

So the soldiers prised open the first cask with their
bayonets. When he saw what was inside, the officer
exclaimed, "Gadzooks! It's Cut-throat Jake! One of
the most villainous scoundrels on the coast!"

Captain Pugwash was too astonished to utter a
word. The Lieutenant turned to him. "As for you,
sir, I owe you an apology, *and* a substantial sum of
money. There's a reward of a thousand crowns on
that ruffian's head. Come, let us take breakfast together
at the inn!"

So, while the soldiers recovered the other
two barrels and hustled Jake and his crew away,
the officer and the Captain, the pirates and
Tom, sat down to an enormous breakfast of
tea and porridge and bacon and eggs . . .

. . . and beef-steak and beer, because
people ate very big breakfasts
in those days. And Captain Pugwash
boasted like anything about his many
exploits.

"I wonder what story he'll tell about *this* one?"
thought Tom. "He hasn't the faintest idea what
really happened!"

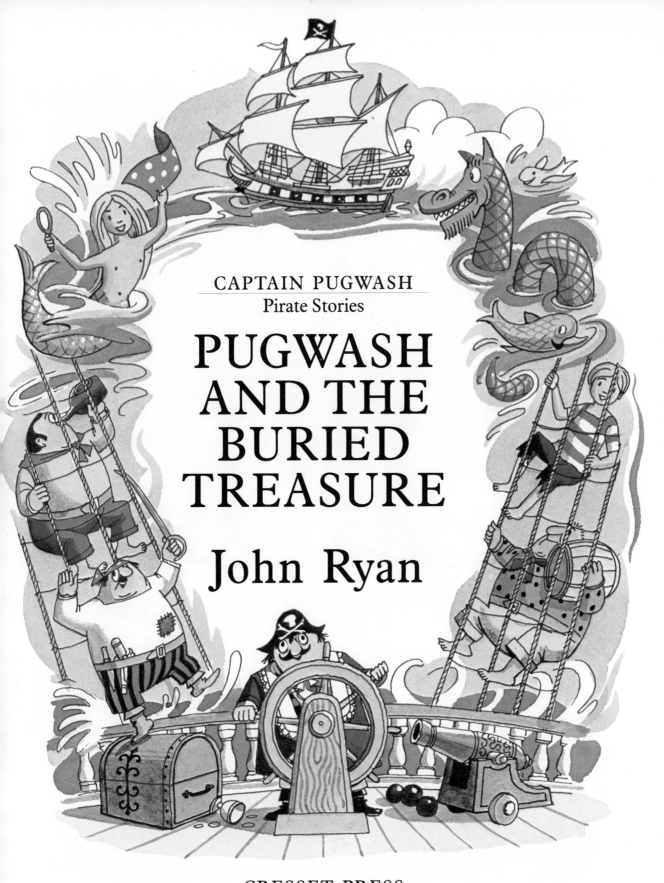

CAPTAIN PUGWASH
Pirate Stories

PUGWASH AND THE BURIED TREASURE

John Ryan

CRESSET PRESS

London Sydney Auckland Johannesburg

It was a dark and stormy night; a great gale blew and the *Black Pig* was tossed high and low by the mountainous waves which broke across the Caribbean Sea.

The pirates were all down below, clinging to their hammocks and feeling dreadfully sea-sick. All, that is, except for two . . .

Tom the cabin boy was up on deck at the wheel, fighting to keep the ship into the wind. And, strangely enough, Captain Pugwash was up there too . . .

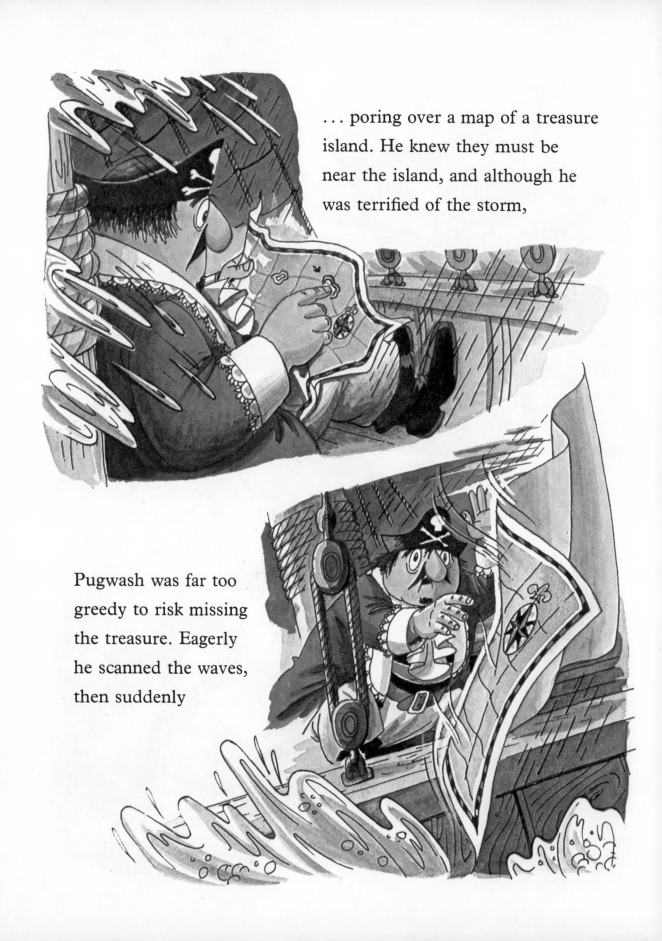

... poring over a map of a treasure island. He knew they must be near the island, and although he was terrified of the storm,

Pugwash was far too greedy to risk missing the treasure. Eagerly he scanned the waves, then suddenly a gust of wind snatched the map from his grasp

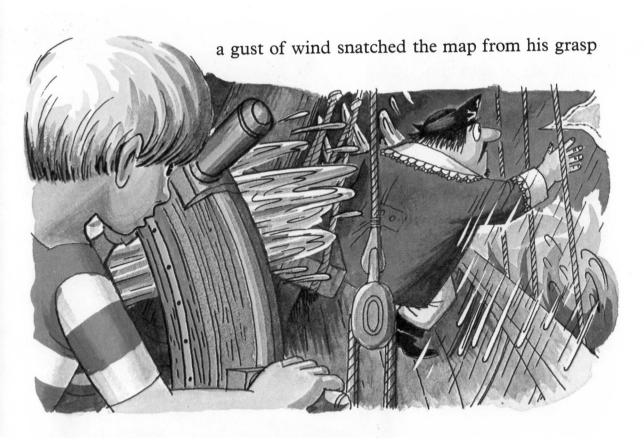

and as he started after it a great wave caught him

and swept him off his feet,

tossing him over the
side of the ship into
the raging waves below.

Poor Captain Pugwash! He hated cold water
and he was a very poor swimmer. And he knew
that in a storm like this even Tom wouldn't be
able to turn the ship back to save him.

By now the *Black Pig* was disappearing into the darkness and Pugwash felt that his last hour really had come. Then all of a sudden . . .

... his hand struck something hard. LAND! It wasn't dry
land but it was at least firm. In the darkness the Captain
could just see the outline of a tiny rocky island.
Desperately he dragged
himself up on to it, and
a moment later ... he fell
into an exhausted sleep.

When the Captain awoke it was dawn. The
terrible storm was over, the sea was dead calm.
And there he sat, all alone on his little island.
Or *was* he alone?

From close by, on the other side of the rock in fact, he heard a snore . . .

... then a loud SNORT. And he knew that snort all too well. He looked round, and yes ... there to his horror and terror

sat his worst and most dreaded enemy, the wickedest and most ferocious pirate on the seven seas, Cut-throat Jake! Then Pugwash got another surprise ...

Cut-throat Jake was smiling!

At first of course the Captain was absolutely *terrified*

but oddly enough, Cut-throat Jake seemed friendly.
He told Pugwash how he too had been swept away
by the storm and cast up on the island.

And very soon the two
pirates were chatting away
just like old friends.

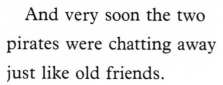

Pugwash even shared his
last bit of sea-watery chocolate
with his old enemy.

At least he *pretended* it
was his last piece of
chocolate, and Cut-throat
Jake *pretended* that he
believed him!

Then, far away on the horizon, they saw a
ship. Both pirates were very excited. "Why, ain't
that lucky now that we've become mates!" said Jake.

"With the two of us it'll be easy to attract their
attention! Take yer jacket off, me handsome!"

Jake stood on the rock
and Pugwash climbed on
to his shoulders and
waved his coat wildly.

And the ship seemed to
be getting closer . . .
and closer . . . and closer,
although in the early
morning light it was
difficult to be
absolutely sure.

Captain Pugwash was beginning to feel rather dizzy so finally both pirates stood hand in hand on their little island and shouted for all they were worth.

Soon the ship was so close that Cut-throat Jake roared with delight and gave a blood-thirsty chuckle. "Why!" he growled, "it's me own ship the *Flyin' Dustman*, and me own shipmates come to save me. Ho, Ho!"

"And me too?" asked Pugwash nervously.

AHOY THERE CAP'N JAKE !

"Save *you*?" roared Jake. "You didn't *believe* all that clap-trap about 'bygones be bygones' did 'ee? That was just to get 'ee to help me make 'em see us! Nay! It's *me* that's for savin' and *you* that's for maroonin' on this 'ere island, aharrh!"

By this time Jake's pirates had arrived in
their long-boat. And a moment later Cut-
throat Jake was being helped aboard.

"B-b-but you can't *leave* me here!" cried Pugwash.

"Why that I can and that I *will*, you old
scallywag," replied Jake.

And he was gone, and very soon the *Flying Dustman* was receding into the distance.

"Come back! Come BACK!" shouted Captain Pugwash. But Jake and his crew only laughed at him. And very soon the Captain couldn't even hear that.

As the hot mid-day sun rose overhead and
Jake's ship disappeared over the eastern horizon,
poor Captain Pugwash gave up all hope. In fact,
he was so hopeless and downcast he never noticed
that over the *western* horizon *another* ship had
arrived.

It was the Captain's ship, the *Black Pig*!

Eagerly the pirates rushed to the side.

In next to no time Tom the cabin boy was on his way to the tiny island in the dinghy. "Well done, Tom lad!" cried Pugwash. "I might have known none of you would rest until you had found your gallant Captain!"

"Well, as a matter of fact," said Tom, "it wasn't *you* we were looking for."

"We found your map after the storm; it was
caught in the rigging. And with the map we found
the island. And as for the treasure Cap'n, why . . .

YOU'VE BEEN SITTING ON IT!"

And sure enough
they found

under the rocks
and sand

an ancient rusty chest,

which was absolutely *stuffed* with treasure!

That night they all had a very merry party
aboard the *Black Pig*. As the pirates played with
the sparkling loot and counted it all up, Captain
Pugwash told them *his* version of the story:

– how he had cleverly spotted the island in the storm, dived into the raging sea, swam ashore and took possession of the island, defending it against Cut-throat Jake, and finally how he had driven off Jake and his entire villainous crew!

"I just don't know *what* you'd do without me," remarked Captain Pugwash later as Tom prepared his bath.

"Hm, I felt we did pretty well on our own," thought Tom, "but even so, it's good to have our Cap'n back again!"

This edition produced in 1992 by Cresset Press
an imprint of the Random Century Group Ltd
Captain Pugwash © John Ryan 1952
Pugwash the Smuggler © John Ryan 1976
Pugwash and the Buried Treasure © John Ryan 1980

Printed and bound in Singapore
by Kim Hup Lee Printing Co Pte Limited
ISBN 0 09 175412 7